P9-CPY-226

HALLY™

ONE SMART COOKIE

BY

SUSAN CAPPADONIA LOVE

COVER ART BY KRISTI VALIANT
STORY ILLUSTRATIONS BY KELLY MURPHY

An Our Generation® *book*

MAISON BATTAT INC. *Publisher*

A very special thanks to the editor,
Joanne Burke Casey.

Our Generation® Books is a registered trademark of Maison Battat Inc.
Text copyright © 2007 by Susan Love
Characters portrayed in this book are fictitious. Any references to historical
events, real people, or real locales are used fictitiously. Other names,
characters, places, and incidents are products of the author's imagination,
and any resemblance to actual events or locales or persons, living or dead,
is entirely coincidental.
All rights reserved, including the right of reproduction in whole or in part
in any form.
ISBN: 978-0-9794542-1-9
Printed in China

our
generation®

This is Hally's story.

For Scott, Sophie and Olivia,
who I have the good fortune
of loving.

Read all the adventures in the
Our Generation® Book Series

One Smart Cookie
featuring Hally™

Blizzard on Moose Mountain
featuring Katelyn™

Stars in Your Eyes
featuring Sydney Lee™

The Note in the Piano
featuring Mary Lyn™

The Mystery of the Vanishing Coin
featuring Eva®

Adventures at Shelby Stables
featuring Lily Anna®

The Sweet Shoppe Mystery
featuring Jenny™

The Jumpstart Squad
featuring Juliet™

The Dress in the Window
featuring Audrey-Ann®

The Jukebox Babysitters
featuring Ashley-Rose®

In the Limelight
featuring Evelyn®

The Most Fantabulous Pajama Party Ever
featuring Willow™

Read more about **Our Generation®** books and dolls online:
ourgeneration.com

TABLE OF CONTENTS

EXTRA! EXTRA! READ ALL ABOUT IT!

*Big words, wacky words, powerful words, funny words...
what do they all mean? They are marked with this symbol * .
Look them up in the Glossary at the end of this book.*

Chapter One

If you think you're too small to make a difference, you haven't been in bed with a mosquito.
—Anita Roddick

"Don't do it, Hally," pleaded my sister, Erin, "pleeeeeaaase don't!"

"You remember what happened when you opened a fortune cookie last year," warned Mrs. Wu.

"And the year before that?" asked my mom.

Ellie tried to snatch my cookie, hoping to prevent disaster*. "Stop!" she shouted in alarm. "Barlafumble!" (My best friend, Ellie Wu, is just crazy for words—the more oddball they are, the more she loves them.)

"Maaaaaaaaybe it's not such a good idea, honey," groaned my dad. Concern was written all over his face.

What was the big fuss all about? It was for good reason.

You might wonder—can a tiny piece of white paper tucked inside a fortune cookie really predict what the future holds?

Just ask me. I'm Hally, and I have plenty of firsthand experience in the fortune cookie department.

You see, every year on the night before the first day of school, Ellie and I go to the Lucky Wow Chow Restaurant with our families. My mom says traditions* like this are important because they celebrate special times in life.

We haven't missed a year yet at the Lucky Wow Chow since Ellie and I started at Pickering Point Kindergarten together. Now we're in fourth grade.

All nine of us sit in the same big round booth every year. There's me, my mom, my dad, Erin, Ellie, her mom and dad and her brother. Plus, there's Ellie's Grandfather Wu,

who my dad describes as *the nicest guy around, but a man of very few words.*

The seats of the booth are covered in shiny red vinyl. There's a lazy Susan* in the middle of the table that holds food and spins, so everyone can share. That way, we can all taste a few dishes instead of just one.

Every year after dinner, the waiter sets a plate of fortune cookies down on the lazy Susan and we give it a whirl around. Here's another tradition: you take the fortune cookie that stops right in front of you.

That's when everyone at the table (except Ellie's grandfather) begs me not to open my fortune cookie.

Because somehow, some way, the same thing happens. I open my cookie and the words on my fortunes spell out what's just around the corner. Trouble. "With a capital T," as Mrs. Wu says. Or as my mother says, "a lesson to be learned by all."

That's because I usually drag other

12

innocent people into my fortune cookie fiascos*, whether they like it or not.

cx/cy

Perfect example: the night before second grade, I cracked open a cookie and the fortune read, "Never Trouble Trouble Till Trouble Troubles You." Oh boy. Talk about trouble. Our school librarian, Mr. Smithwick, will never let me forget it.

I had convinced the reading club to sort the fiction* books by the colors of the rainbow. The shelves looked beautiful when we finished, if I do say so myself. First came the red covers, followed by a burst of orange, a splash of yellow, a gorgeous section of green, then blue melting into indigo and finally lovely violet last.

When Mr. Smithwick spotted the shelves, he took a startled step back and blinked. Then he leaned his head forward real slow and his eyes got all squinty.

He seemed absolutely amazed. I took this as a sign that he thought the shelves were beautiful, too. *Wrong.*

He slowly swiveled his head toward me and spoke very quietly, through clenched teeth. "Should I bother to ask who is behind all of this? No. I think not." He took a deep breath and lifted himself up straight and tall.

"And *why* did you think it was a good idea to sort the books like this?" he asked.

"Well, we're studying rainbows in Mrs. Dimp's science class," I said.

Being the true-blue* friend that she is, Ellie tried to take some of the bad attention off of me. "That's Red, Orange, Yellow, Green, Blue, Indigo and Violet," she said. "The colors of the rainbow are easy to remember if you just remember the first letter of each of these words: Ratting On Your Grumpy Brother Is Vile*."

"I see. Well, I do hope that you are free on Saturday morning, Hally. Because that is when you and your "Rainbow Club" will put every single book back in alphabetical order according to the author's last name."

The Rainbow Club. Hmmm...I liked the sound of it.

"Just like they were before," he continued, "just like they are supposed to be. And *will be*, by Saturday afternoon."

I can see now that sorting the books without permission wasn't the best idea I've ever had. But remember, I was only seven then, and I was in my artistic phase.

As my dad later said, raising his eyebrows and sighing, "if you didn't take the trouble to arrange 192 books by colors, trouble would not have troubled you."

My mom, however, had a positive attitude about it. "Just look at all the good books you found to read."

Another good thing came out of it, too. All 11 kids in the newly named Rainbow Club sure did get the hang of alphabetizing by the time we put all those books back.

That happened so long ago. And yes, there had been other cookie misfortunes since. But this was a new year. I couldn't let my life be ruled by superstitions*, could I?

No way. I threw caution to the wind, cracked that cookie open and read the piece of paper that was tucked inside.

Oh my.

Chapter Two

The road ahead can be bumpy, but don't fret about the potholes.

When I opened this year's fortune cookie, I pretended that I was not at all concerned. And when I read the six words inside, I pretended even harder. Here's why:

Life had been going along just swell. Great. Nearly perfect.

I had brand new sneakers to wear on the first day of school.

I knew almost all of the kids in my class.

My backpack was fully stocked.

Stuff for My Backpack

☑ 6 sharp #2 pencils and a life-sized nose pencil sharpener

☑ big eraser in the shape of an ice cream cone

☑ sparkly notebook with a zippered pocket for pencils

☑ folder with a puppy on the front

☑ my lucky 1999 penny

☑ a keychain clip with a mini compass

Plus, this year I had the best teacher in school, Ms. Mann. Everyone said she even made schoolwork fun.

For example, each day Ms. Mann put a brainteaser on the chalkboard. Each kid in the class could write answers to the riddles on a piece of paper and put it into a cookie jar shaped like a great big brain. After lunch, she'd reach her hand into the jar and pull out an answer. If it was correct, the winner got to skip classroom chores that day.

So you see, things just couldn't have been

better. That's why it made me nervous when I read my Lucky Wow Chow fortune:

Things Aren't Always What They Seem. 😊

Calm down, I thought. *No biggie.* Everyone knows that statement is true. For instance, one minute it might be raining cats and dogs and the next minute the sun comes out and it's a perfect afternoon for a bike ride.

Or my basketball team might be losing 23 to 24 with 8 seconds left in the game—then I dribble up the court, sink a basket and win the game. The crowd leaps to their feet in the bleachers, wildly clapping and chanting my name—"Hally, Hally, Hally—"

Mrs. Wu's voice shook me out of my very exciting basketball daydream. She was pointing at my fortune. "Here comes Trouble," she said, "with a capital T."

19

"*Muy loco en la cabeza,*" said Erin, tapping her skull, "you're crazy in the head."

"You've really done it now," said Ellie, smacking her forehead with her hand. "Why do you have to be such a fopdoodle?"

"What's a fopdoodle?" asked my dad.

"A silly-billy," said Ellie.

"What's a silly-billy?" asked Mr. Wu, who is Ellie's dad.

"A foolish person," said Ellie. "No offense, Hally. You're still my bestest-ever boonfellow." That's one word I knew by heart, because it means good friend.

I laughed and said they were *all* being silly-billies and fopdoodles. But when Ellie went to the bathroom, I munched on my cookie and looked at the fortune again.

Those six words should have tipped me off. Because right then, "things" were a little too hunky-dory*.

I put the fortune in the pocket of my jacket. *Don't be silly,* I thought, *there's nothing to worry about.*

Sure enough, just like clockwork*, "things" started to get a little crazy.

Chapter Three

Teachers open doors,
but you must enter by yourself.

I sat back in my brand new desk in the third row. I admired my extra-white, just-out-of-the-box sneakers and wiggled my toes around. They were just a little big so that we "don't have to buy another pair next week" because I'm "growing faster than grass" as my mom says. I looked around and saw my teacher, the best teacher in the school, writing something on the board.

Today's Brainteaser:
What are three-letter words for:
1. the sound of a bursting balloon?
2. a joke?
3. what you see with?

Hint, hint: The answers are palindromes.
Look that word up in your dictionary.

I opened my dictionary. Flip-flip-flip, L...M...N...O...P! I found the Ps. The whole class was rifling* through their dictionary pages like crazy. Aha! There was the word I was looking for—palindrome: a word or phrase that is spelled the same way backward as it is forward. Hmmm...interesting.

"Bingo," whispered Frankie. He'd found the definition, too.

Then no one said a word. All the kids in my class were using their noodles* to find the answers to the riddle. I looked around the classroom.

Louise was tapping her pencil eraser on the desk.

Frankie was looking at the board, squinting, and his tongue was peeking a little outside the corner of his mouth.

Ellie was staring into space with real concentration on her face. If anyone could get

all three answers correct, it was Ellie. Weird words, words no one has spoken in five hundred years, crossword puzzles, Scrabble® games, spelling bees—if it had to do with words, it was right up her alley.

I got cooking on the Brainteaser. I had #1 figured out right off the bat (it was *pop*). But #2 and #3 were harder. (You can figure them out, too, and check your answers at the end of this book.)

The last bell rang and it was officially

official. The first day of fourth grade had ended. I could feel it. It was going to be my best school year yet.

"Wait a second, everyone," said Ms. Mann. "I want you to begin thinking about a homework assignment. Come up with a question you've always wondered about, research the answer and give a three-minute speech."

A speech? How could Ms. Mann do this to me? I thought she was supposed to be the best teacher in the whole school.

"On October 5th—that's three weeks from now—everyone will give their speeches in front of the class."

A speech in front of 26 people? Who are staring at you and only you? It's one thing to talk and goof around with your classmates on the playground. It's another thing entirely to talk to them from the front of the class. That's serious business.

It felt like there was a thunder and lightning storm booming in my head. My

25

stomach felt swirly-whirly.

I glanced at Ellie in the first row. She was looking at me and frowning with her bottom lip stuck out, like "I know you're aglifft and getting a major woofits (which means frightened and getting a headache). Don't worry. It will be OK."

I knew she was trying to make me feel better. But I didn't think it would be OK. Just hearing the word "speech" gave me butterflies in my stomach.

"Anyone who gets a B grade or above," added Ms. Mann, "will be able to go on the field trip to the Wild and Woolly Mammoth* Exhibit at the Museum of Natural History."

I *really really really* wanted to see the Wild and Woolly Mammoth Exhibit.

"Are we riding on the luxury bus with the high seats covered in the crazy fabric?" asked Louise. "The one that has a teeny-tiny bathroom in the back with an itty-bitty sink?"

"That's the one," said Ms. Mann.

"Wow!" Ellie exclaimed.

"Did you know that's a palindrome?" Ms. Mann asked.

"Huh?" Ellie wondered aloud.

"That's a palindrome, too," said Ms. Mann. "Wow and huh are each spelled the same backward as they are forward."

"Aha!" said Ellie. Now she was getting the hang of palindromes.

"Three in a row—my, my, you really have

a knack for this, Ellie."

But back to the luxury bus with high fabric seats and the bathroom in the back. It was so cool. We rode on it last year when we went to the Textiles of Yesterday and Today Museum. That field trip was so much fun. We used looms and saw how fleece was made.

Gary raised his hand. "What if you *don't* get a B or above?"

"Anyone who puts time into their research and presents an interesting speech will get a B, Gary. But anyone who doesn't will take a special research class with the librarian, Mr. Smithwick, while the others are at the exhibit." That was all I needed to hear. I absolutely had to find the Courage to do this speech.

Courage is a tricky thing, though. Before you can use it, you must have it. And right now my Courage was hiding—under a whole pile of Stage Fright*.

Chapter Four

What are you waiting for?
Express yourself.

The second week of school Ms. Mann announced that "It's Celebrate Poetry Week!" The reaction in class was less enthusiastic.

Ughh, I thought, *what an awful, boring week this is going to be.*

Frankie slumped his shoulders and sighed. Louise rolled her eyes and began doodling on the cover of her notebook.

Gary made a face like the lunch lady just plopped Mystery Casserole onto his tray. Mystery Casserole is no mystery. It's Friday's school cafeteria lunch made from Monday-Tuesday-Wednesday-Thursday leftovers. Be afraid, be very afraid. Better yet, pack your lunch on Fridays.

Only Ellie the word lover looked thrilled, like she had just won the lottery.

Ms. Mann explained that poetry is just another way of telling a story. She said a poem can be about sports, a vacation, your pet or even a dream you had last night. "You name it," she said, "and you can write a poem about it."

Louise raised her hand and waved it around like mad to get Ms. Mann's attention. "Could you, for example," she asked, "write a poem about someone who's always hogging the ball in soccer?"

Ellie instantly shot her a look, knowing that comment was about her. "That's poppycock! Balderdash!" (meaning nonsense!) she said. Her lips were all bunched up and she was wagging her finger at Louise. "What a blob-tale!" she muttered under her breath. (Blob-tale meaning tattletale, of course.)

This was not the first time we've heard this complaint. In fact, it's been a never-ending

sore spot between these two for a couple of years. But I'm not sure why. They're both really nice people.

For instance, Ellie is one of the very kindest people I know. We had just volunteered together collecting new backpacks, pencils, notebooks, pens and granola bars. The backpacks were delivered to homeless shelters so the kids who stay there would have backpacks and supplies for the first day of school.

Louise has a good heart, too. Every week, she and her mom do the grocery shopping for a neighbor who can't drive anymore. Louise also reads the mail to her neighbor because her eyesight isn't as good as it used to be.

"Writing is a great way to let off steam about whatever is on your mind," said Ms. Mann. "It lets you express your feelings."

Gary spoke out of turn, without raising his hand. "A feeling like being grumpy for two whole weeks and taking it out on your best friend?"

Frankie stayed in the slumping position. But his eyes darted to the left toward Gary and his ears moved up and down. He does that when he's mad, but I can't figure out how.

"Certainly," said our teacher. "But poems can also be funny." She smiled to herself. "I wonder...have you ever tasted a poem sandwich?"

It's bad enough, I thought, *that we have to read and write poems all week. But now we have to eat them, too? Blah!*

"That's what a limerick is—it's like a poem sandwich. It has three long lines that rhyme with each other on the top and bottom. There are two short lines that rhyme in the middle." She wrote a limerick on the chalkboard to show us an example:

Writing a limerick is not that hard to do,
It has five lines that get a laugh or two.
Put two short lines that rhyme,
Between three long lines each time,
And you'll find a poet lives inside of you.

"Pick your own subject. Inspiration* is all around you. You just have to look." Then she told us to get to work creating our own limericks.

I finished my limerick PDQ (Pretty Darn Quick) and looked around the room. A few kids were writing and silently giggling at their own poems.

I was surprised. Poetry wasn't as bad as I thought. In fact, it was pretty silly—and fun. I guess things *aren't* always what they seem.

Interesting...just like my fortune said. *Who thought up the idea of fortune cookies anyway?* I thought. *Hey, there's my question for the speech I hope I never have to give.*

Researching the assignment would be interesting. It was the speech that made me nervous.

When ten minutes was up, Ms. Mann was smiling like a proud parent whose child had just won a medal.

"I must say, I'm very impressed. You have all been working so hard on this limerick assignment. I can tell you put your whole heart into it. Looks like we'll have very creative poetry to hang on the wall for Parents' Night next week. Would anyone like to share theirs before class ends?"

I crossed my pointer and middle fingers under the desk for luck and protection. *Not me,* I thought to myself, *don't call on me.*

Chapter Five

Whether you think you can,
or you can't, you are usually right.
—Henry Ford

Ms. Mann glanced at me, but saw that Gary's hand had shot up and was wiggling all five fingers. She asked him to read his poem in the front of the class.

Phew!

"H–h-h-hhm," he cleared his throat and glanced quickly at Frankie.

There once was a fourth-grader named
Frankie,
I don't know why he was acting so cranky.
He was super grumpy at school,
He called me a toad and a fool,
And his behavior lately is stinky-stanky.

"Hey," snapped Frankie, his ears quickly moving up and down.

"Now, now," said Ms. Mann, "Frankie is a very well-behaved student."

"That's right," Frankie muttered. "Bingo."

Louise raised her hand and was called on next:

There once was a girl name Ellie Wu,
Who always stole the soccer ball from you.
Gym class wasn't fun or fair,
Because she wouldn't share
With other players and it makes me stew*.

Ellie fumed. "Hogwash. What a bunch of flimflam." (Meaning there was no truth to it.) A few people tittered*. I blew a "phfff" of air to defend Ellie. She looked at me and mouthed the words *"hufty-tufty."* (Which of course, meant Louise was annoying and acting like a show-off.)

Ms. Mann was not pleased. Her eyes

scanned the room. "Tut-tut," she scolded.

"Hey, that's a palindrome!" Ellie blurted.

Ms. Mann changed into her find-something-happy-about-this-situation face.

From day one in her class she had said: "If a situation looks gloomy, try to pick out one good thing about it, even if you have to dig through a lot of bad things to find it." That's just what she did then.

"You certainly did look around you for inspiration. And your rhyming is excellent," she praised. "But tomorrow I think we'll draw topics out of a hat and see what we can come up with for Parents' Night."

"Wait until you hear my speech," said Frankie, while we were waiting at the bus stop. "It's all about yawning."

"That sounds *so* exciting," said Gary, writing his name in the dirt with his shoe. "If

I can stay awake for those three minutes, I'm sure your speech will have me on the edge of my seat."

"Call it the Sloomy Speech," said Ellie. "Sloomy means sleepy."

"Why do you have to make up weird words all the time?" groaned Gary.

Ellie was offended and hurt. "I don't make them up and they're not weird," she protested. "A long time ago those were popular words that people used all the time. But new words came along and kind of replaced them."

"So use the new ones and you won't sound like such an oddball."

"Don't talk like a chucklehead," said Ellie, using her polite word for a person who's not being all that smart. "If no one uses them, they'll be forgotten forever. They're like antiques—they have value because they're old and interesting."

"Speaking of words like sloomy," I said, "hey Frankie, are you going to answer the

mystery about why yawning is contagious*?"

"Bingo," said Frankie, "plus a lot more. For example, do you know how many seconds the average yawn is? Or how many times a day people yawn?"

"How many seconds?" Louise asked, while giving Ellie a ring she had woven from colorful gum wrappers. She was still feeling a little sorry for writing that limerick.

Ellie smiled. "Thank you, bellibone. I forgive you for being a chattermucker." (Meaning Louise was no longer a hufty-tufty and blob-tale and she was now a nice, lovely girl.)

"How many times?" Gary asked, looking interested now.

"I can't tell you now," said Frankie, "I guess you'll have to stay awake during my speech."

"I just thought of a limerick for Frankie's Sloomy Speech," I said.

A silly girl once jumped rope all night,
The next day her yawns were quite a sight,
When her mouth opened wide,
A passing fly flew inside
We don't know who had more of a fright.

"Bingo," Frankie said, "that's so good."

I'll be honest. I hadn't put much of a dent* in my research for the speech. I had printed out some good information such as a fortune cookie recipe.

Also, I have every fortune from every cookie that I've ever eaten. I planned on making a poster board with those, since Ms. Mann said we could use visual aids*. And I had put two books on hold at the library about fortune cookies. They were supposed to come in this week. So there was a little progress*, but not much.

I was panicky just thinking about giving the speech and was avoiding doing the work. In the back of my mind, I knew I'd better get going. I had just seven days left.

Wait a minute. I had an idea.

What if I did all the research and wrote the speech, but was sick on October 5th? I'd bring in my written speech and poster board to show Ms. Mann the next day. She would see that I had done all the work and would

42

probably still let me go to the Wild and Woolly Mammoth Exhibit. Problem solved.

Phew. Things aren't always what they seem, I thought, *sometimes they're a whole lot better.*

I looked at the board again:

Today's Brainteasers:

What are four-, five- and seven-letter palindromes for:

1. a word meaning "look"?
2. a canoe first made by the Eskimos?
3. an auto that goes fast?

Use your noggin*!

I had figured out #2 because I paddled around in one at camp last summer. Ms. Mann got the attention of the class before I figured out the others. (Figure them out for yourself, and check your answers at the end of this book.)

Ms. Mann dipped her hand into the brain cookie jar. She pulled out Gary's paper. All three of his answers were correct.

"Now I won!" Gary said.

Ms. Mann grinned. "You might not believe this, but—"

"'Now I won' is a palindrome, Gary," Ellie blurted out. You could almost see the wheels in everyone's heads turning, then thinking *oh yeah, it is.*

"Good work, Ellie. Now, just a reminder to you all about the speech that's due on October 5th. That's just seven days away."

Don't remind me, I thought.

"To find the answer to the question you

44

picked, you can do research using any resources that are available to you. Read books and magazines, use the Internet, interview people or visit a museum.

"Also, for anyone who is sick that day, you will be able to do your speech on your next day back to school."

Oh, phooey. Now what was I going to do?

"Everyone will a get a chance to speak, so don't worry."

I was worried alright. *Plenty* worried.

Chapter Six

There's a surprise in store for you.

"But Mom, I have a whole week to work on that speech."

"I'm sorry, Hally. You can't go over to Ellie's to play Scrabble® until I've seen more progress on that assignment."

Then I came up with a brainstorm that was pure brilliance. Really, sometimes I surprise myself with such quick thinking.

"One of the reasons I'm going over to Ellie's is to talk to her Grandfather Wu. He moved to the United States from China after college, so I thought I'd interview him about fortune cookies."

"Well..." My mom thought it over. She

had to admit it was a pretty good idea. But I had to admit I had thought it up on the spot so that I could go over to Ellie's house to play.

"Also, Ms. Mann said we could use any resources that were available to us."

"OK," she said, "Ellie's Grandfather Wu is a very smart man. I bet he'll have some good insight into your assignment."

❧ ❧

When I rang Ellie's doorbell, Mrs. Wu opened the door. "Hi, Hally. Your mom just called to say you'd be coming over to interview Grandfather Wu. That's wonderful. I know he'd like the company. Let me go upstairs and get him."

So much for playing with Ellie. I took off my shoes and sweatshirt and put them in the front hall. Ellie popped her head around the corner.

"My boonfellow!" she said with a smile

on her face.

Mrs. Wu and Ellie's Grandfather Wu came down the stairs.

"Hally is here to interview your grandfather for her speech, Ellie. How about you and I start dinner and they can start the project?"

Ellie's smile disappeared as she turned and followed her mom to the kitchen.

I felt awkward when Ellie's grandfather and I sat down in the living room.

I hadn't really talked much with Ellie's Grandfather Wu before. He was always very quiet. I figured he just didn't want to be bothered with kids or maybe he was just grumpy. Plus, I don't have any grandparents who are still living and I didn't know any people who were older.

Truthfully, for the seven months that her grandfather had lived with Ellie, I hadn't been all that friendly to him. I'd said hello and that's about it.

But now I was asking him for something. Information and help. Since he was doing me a favor, I began by saying thank you. He nodded once and smiled a little.

I told him that I knew he had once lived in China, and since fortune cookies were Chinese, I figured he'd know their history.

There was a twinkle in his eyes, like he was up to some kind of mischief. "Things aren't always what they seem."

"Right. That was my fortune." I did not catch his drift.

"It's true that was your fortune, but it's also true about fortune cookies," he said.

"Are you saying...?"

He actually broke out into a big grin.

Where did Ellie's Grumpy Grandfather Wu go? Who was this riddler sitting in front of me. And what in the world was he talking about?

"Chinese fortune cookies aren't Chinese," he said, "they're as American as apple pie!"

I couldn't believe my ears. "Are you pulling my leg?"

I must have had a completely confused expression on my face, because Ellie's Grandfather Wu began chuckling. He imitated the look on my face, then laughed even harder.

He was acting like a kid. Not a grumpy old man. In fact, he looked ridiculous, which was, I guess, just the way I must have looked. I laughed, too. Then I considered the idea that fortune cookies aren't even Chinese. How *silly*.

It was so silly that when Ellie and her mom walked into the room, they were amazed at what they saw. Ellie's grandfather and I were out of control, with our hands over our mouths, rocking back and forth in hysterics, slapping our thighs.

"Stop, stop," I said. "Oh, my stomach hurts. *Barlafumble!*"

And that set us off again in a fit of laughter. Ellie and her mom just shook their heads and went back into the kitchen.

When I left that night, Grandfather Wu said I could come back on Tuesday and we'd

finish the interview.

⊱ ⊰

The next day, before school started, Ellie asked me what all the hullabaloo (noisy racket) had been about.

"Your grandfather is *so* funny," I said.

"Grandfather Wu?" she asked, like she hadn't heard me right.

Then Louise interrupted. "Hally, can you make a limerick up for me? I want to put it into my speech. I'm answering the question 'Why do kangaroos have pouches?'"

"Let me think," I said. A lot of words rhyme with kangaroo, so it was a cinch to come up with a poem. "OK, here goes."

There once was a baby kangaroo,
He begged, "Momma, take me, too."
So she stashed him in her pocket,
And they took off like a rocket,
To visit friends in Kalamazoo.

"Hooray," she whooped. "I'll tell everyone

that you, the Limerick Whiz, wrote it. Now my speech is totally done. I'm so excited."

Wow. She's done? And excited to give her speech?

Here I was, no closer to finding the Courage I needed. It was still in hiding—under that big pile of Stage Fright.

Plus I was just starting my assignment. The question I picked was a flop. I had this big idea of finding out some really interesting Chinese history about fortune cookies and how they were brought to America. Then I found out fortune cookies aren't really from China at all.

Is good fortune in my future? Or is this how the cookie crumbles?

Chapter Seven

The only sure thing about luck is that it will surely change.

"Let me get this straight," I asked Grandfather Wu when we met at the library. "Even though you get fortune cookies in Chinese restaurants, they're actually an American invention*?"

"Pretty much," he said. "But there's more to the story. Their origins* are somewhat mysterious."

A mystery, I thought, *now that sounds interesting.*

"Look what it says in this book."

Sure enough, everything Grandfather Wu had told me was correct. In a nutshell*, someone began making fortune cookies in the

United States sometime around the early 1900s. Who was that someone? That is the real mystery.

Some people believe it was Japanese inventor Makoto Hagiwara who first served fortune cookies in San Francisco's Japanese Tea Garden. Others say a man named David Jung created them to advertise his Hong Kong Noodle Company in Los Angeles, California.

People can't even agree on when the first fortune cookies appeared. Was it in 1914? 1918? 1920? No one can say for sure.

I read aloud from the book. "'Even though fortune cookies are an American tradition, it looks like they might have links to China or Japan. In the 13th and 14th centuries, the Chinese put secret messages into moon cakes. In Japan, people gave and received rice crackers called sembei (pronounced sem-bay) with sayings inside.' This is good stuff to put into the speech."

"Tomorrow, let's take a look at who wrote these fortunes you've collected," Grandfather

Wu said.

"I'm sure they were said by Confucius, the wise Chinese philosopher*," I replied.

"Think so?" There was that sparkle in his eyes. "Think again."

"Don't tell me, don't tell me," I said, rolling my eyes, "things aren't always what they seem?"

"You said it, not me." He started laughing.

"Don't get me started," I began to giggle.

The next day, right before class, Ellie skipped over to my desk, her long black hair bouncing up and down.

"Hi Ellie," I said. "How's your speech coming along?"

"Not that great," she whispered so Ms. Mann wouldn't hear. "What a nincompoop (foolish person) I am. I picked the question: why do bagels have holes? The answer is so simple it will only take me about a minute to explain it...and that's including the limerick I was hoping you'd write. How's yours?"

"I'm having the opposite problem. Too *much* information. I don't even want to give a speech, let alone a three-minute speech. But I think you could fill up six minutes talking about fortune cookies."

"Why don't you take two of my minutes then, since I don't need them?" We both laughed. Then Ellie asked, "Do you want to come over after school?"

"I can't," I said. "Grandfather Wu is meeting me at the library again."

First she looked surprised. Then she looked furious. "You mean *my* Grandfather Wu!" She whirled around in a huff and went to her desk.

What was that all about? I thought. *What did I do to make her so angry?* I had just hurt my best friend's feelings. The very nicest, kindest person I knew.

While I was doing my spelling homework that night, my dad came into my room. He always comes in to chat before he leaves to teach night classes. He's a professor at a college that's close by.

"Well, I understand you have a new friend," he said as he sat down on my bed. "I ran into Ellie's grandfather at the college today."

"Really? What was he doing there?"

"He's a volunteer tutor in the computer lab. Any student who's having difficulty can come in and get help for free."

I had no idea.

"The college is especially lucky to have him as a tutor—he owned a computer company in California, you know. He was a bigwig*. Really knows his stuff."

"Why did he move here?"

"He retired, sold his business, and then... his wife, Ellie's grandmother, died. Mr. and Mrs. Wu convinced him to move into their house so he would be close to them."

I got a gloomy feeling.

I thought about how, before I got to know Grandfather Wu, he was super quiet and it seemed to me that he didn't want to be bothered with kids. But maybe he was sad. Or lonely. Or both.

I had also figured he was crabby. But that couldn't have been further from the truth. He

was smart and funny and helped people, just like Ellie. *I guess friends come in all ages*, I thought.

"Anyway, he said he's glad to make a friend like you in Pickering Point. And he said that your fortune cookie project is going to be great. So good he wishes he could be there when you make the speech to your class."

As soon as my dad started talking about

me actually standing in front of the class and giving my speech, I got that panicky feeling all over again.

I was sweating. My stomach felt swirly-whirly. My head felt big and heavy like a bowling ball. More than ever, I felt like I just couldn't get up my nerve to give a speech.

Maybe I'd stumble over my words. Or I'd forget what I was going to say.

Chances are, my face would get all red and blotchy the way it always does when I'm nervous. Then everyone would laugh at me. I'd be a huge failure.

Chapter Eight

The only way to have a friend is to be one.
—Ralph Waldo Emerson

Today's Brainteasers:

Find the answers to these riddles.

1. My doctor was once a (center of the eye) (student).
2. Uncle (name) paid the restaurant (check).
3. All that (herb) gum is worth a (fortune).

Hint, hint: Use the (clues). The answers are homographs.

Look that word up in your dictionary.

I heard kids wildly flipping through their dictionaries. We played the homograph game once when we drove to Florida. So I knew that a homograph is two words that are written the same way but have different meanings. (They're fun to do, so try it out and check your answers at the end of this book.)

I stared at the chalkboard. I could hardly concentrate on the riddle, because my brain was working overtime on a few other riddles.

For example, I knew that I hadn't been spending much time with Ellie because I was spending a lot of time with Grandfather Wu. I could tell she was miffed and hurt. Riddle #1: How was I going to fix this situation?

Also, the speech was a big project. I had put it off for too long. Time was running out. And Grandfather Wu said he'd help, but of course, I had to do the real work myself or it would be like cheating. Riddle #2: How would I get it done in time?

Plus, there was just too much information on fortune cookies to fit into a three-minute speech. Riddle #3: What could I cut out to make it shorter? All the stories and facts were interesting.

Which brings me to Riddle #4: Even if I did get my speech ready in time, how was I ever going to get up in front of all those kids? I got dizzy every time I thought about it.

I remembered Ms. Mann's plan of action for those times when things just weren't working out: "If a situation looks gloomy, try to pick out one good thing about it, even if you have to dig through a lot of bad things to find it."

I decided to try it out. There was one good thing I could do to patch things up with Ellie.

❧ ❧

The cafeteria on Thursdays was always crazy. It was pizza day which most kids like. But Ellie and I always pack our lunches, so we were sitting at our lunch table while everyone else was still in line. I couldn't stop fidgeting.

"Why are you jiffling like that?" Ellie asked.

"Um, I was thinking about that limerick for your speech. How's this sound?"

There once was a woman from Idaho,
Who wanted a diamond ring for her big toe.
But the jeweler sold her instead,
A garlic bagel of white bread,
Because he didn't think she had enough dough.

That put a flicker of a smile on her face. "That's funny. I wish I could use it."

"Why can't you?"

"I gave the speech to my mom and she timed it. It was just about a minute and a half. That means I might not get a good grade. And I *really* want to go to that exhibit. So I'll have to spend this weekend preparing a new speech."

"That stinks. What's your new question?" Ellie looked glum. "I don't know. I wish I had a good one like yours."

"Geez, yours is too short and mine's too long. You have to work all weekend and so do I.

I still have a ton of research and writing to do."

We looked at each other. And smiled. "Are you thinking what I'm thinking?"

"Great minds think alike. Right after lunch, let's go ask Ms. Mann if we can combine our speeches!"

We gave each other a high-five over our PB and J sandwiches.

Ms. Mann gave us a thumb's up on working together for our speech. "But," she said, "it will have to be doubly good since two of you are working on it."

After school, Ellie and I met Grandfather Wu at the library and got right to work looking up where some of the fortunes on the poster board came from.

Ellie went on the Internet. I went through books filled with famous sayings called quotations. Grandfather Wu made suggestions when we asked for help and read the newspaper when we were busy.

We couldn't find out who said some of the fortunes, but many of them we could. And what we discovered surprised both of us.

Remember how certain I was that Confucius had said what was on all those fortunes? He was wise, that's for sure. And so were a whole lot of other people. For example:

> Never trouble trouble
> till trouble troubles you.

John Adams, who was the second President of the United States, said that.

> Everyone is kneaded out of the same dough
> but not baked in the same oven.

This is a Yiddish* proverb*.

> Great thoughts come from the heart.

This is wisdom by Luc de Clapiers, a French writer.

Please all and you will please none.

This is from Aesop, a Greek storyteller (6th century B.C.).

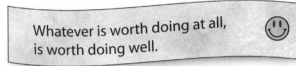

Whatever is worth doing at all, is worth doing well.

Philip Dormer Stanhope, Earl of Chesterfield, who was from England, said this.

What you think you become.

That was by Buddha (563–483 B.C.), a religious leader of India and founder of Buddhism.

Once again, we found, things aren't always what they seem. Wise people around the world said what was printed on the fortunes.

When Grandfather Wu was driving us home from the library, Ellie got a gleam in her eyes. Like grandfather, like granddaughter. I could tell she was cooking up something very big. I had no idea how big, though.

"I think we need to get the kids' attention," Ellie said. "Something to *knock their socks off.* You've done a lot of work already, Hally. How about if I work on this? Trust me, it will be fantastic."

This was Ellie talking—of course it would be fantastic.

"Sure, surprise me," I answered.

It was a surprise all right. An *enormous* surprise.

Chapter Nine

Hear with your ears,
but listen with your heart.

I was playing tetherball with Ellie when we overheard Gary and Frankie arguing.

Out of the corner of my eye, I saw Gary with his hands on his hips shouting at Frankie who was pointing his finger and moving his ears up and down. It went something like this:

Gary: "Did too!" Frankie: "Did *not*." Gary: "Did too!" Frankie: "Did *not*."

You get the picture. This went on for quite awhile. Then:

Gary: "Anyway, Hally isn't the only limerick writer around here. I came up with one of my own. Listen to this."

*For weeks this kid Frankie was in a
grumpy mood,
As a dinner guest he was terribly rude,
He left nothing for the host,
Except a crumb of burnt toast,
And when she went to eat it, he snatched it
and booed.*

Frankie: "*Hey*, my mom says I have excellent table manners."

Ellie: "Guys, c'mon. Cool it. Gary, why don't you just ask Frankie what's bugging him?"

Me: "Yeah, then you can both just get over it, once and for all."

Gary: "*Fine*. What's bugging you? Why are you in such a bad mood lately?"

Frankie: (He was kicking at the dirt and his ears were bobbing up and down.) "Mary Alice Jenkins told everybody on the bus that you said I called her little sister a real cottonbrain."

Gary: "I *never ever in a million years* said that."

Frankie: "She told me that when I get to middle school, I'm really in for it, because her BIG sister is just waiting for me. And then...." (He sliced his hand across his throat, like well, you get the picture.)

Gary: "I'll prove I never said that. Really. C'mon. There she is. We'll go ask her right now."

Frankie: "Really? You didn't tell her that?"

Gary: "Frankie, you're my best friend. Since like we were kids. First of all, you'd never say something mean like that. And second of all, I wouldn't repeat it if you did."

Frankie: "OK. Big mistake. Sorry." (His ears were completely still.)

Me: "Group hug, everybody."

Gary: (smiling slyly at Frankie) "Great idea, Hally."

As soon as we dropped the tetherball to group hug, Gary and Frankie rushed in and started playing.

Well, you win some and you lose some.

"I guess they *honeyfuggled* us," sighed

Ellie (meaning they had tricked us).

We bounced a Mile-High Bounce Ball back and forth and talked about the speech.

"I didn't mean to make you mad before, Ellie, and I'm sorry."

"It wasn't really you who made me angry, Hally. I was being a glump and a fuzzdutty." (A pouting grump and silly person.)

"Hmmm?"

"Grandfather Wu used to live pretty far away, so I didn't know him all that well," Ellie said. "And I guess I didn't realize that he was lonely when he moved here. I didn't see that he was smart and funny and...not until I saw you two laughing hysterically that night, that is."

"So you don't mind that I call him Grandfather Wu? Or that he's helping us with the project?"

"No way. I'm happy. And I can see he's happy. And he's really helped us. In fact, I had a little idea I wanted to run by you."

There was that gleam in her eyes again.

"You know how we're making those fortune cookies this weekend? While we're passing them out during the speech, we really could use someone to read that tall tale about fortune cookies—"

"Great idea, Ellie. Ask Grandfather Wu if he'll be our guest speaker. He'll have the kids in stitches." I thought for a second. "You're pretty lucky, you know?"

"Yes, I am, my boonfellow, in more ways than one." She beamed at me. "Oh, I almost forgot. Grandfather Wu asked me to give this to you."

I took the tiny slip of white paper from the palm of her hand. It read:

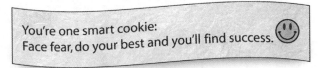

You're one smart cookie:
Face fear, do your best and you'll find success. 😊

"You can do it, Hally," Ellie said. She put her arm around me and we skipped into school. When I put my Mile-High Bounce Ball back into my pocket, my fingers touched something crinkly. It was my fortune from the Lucky Wow Chow Restaurant.

I looked at it and wondered, *Can a tiny piece of white paper tucked inside a fortune cookie really predict what the future holds?*

Let's review the day's events:

Frankie wasn't in a bad mood *or* mad at Gary. He just had bad information and hurt feelings.

Gary didn't want a group hug. He wanted to play tetherball.

And sometimes when someone, even a special boonfellow, acts upset with you, it's not because you've done something *wrong*—it's because you've done something *right*.

Yep, things aren't always what they seem.

I looked at the fortune Grandfather Wu had given to me. With all my heart, I wanted to face my fear of speaking in front of the class. I had three days. Three days to drag the Stage Fright out to the garbage can so I could find the Courage that had been hiding underneath it.

Could I do it in time? SOS!

Chapter Ten

Well done is better than well said.
—Ben Franklin

"Which do you want first? The good news or the bad news?" Ellie asked when she came over to my house on Saturday to bake cookies.

"Bad news, I guess."

"The big surprise? It was a big flop—literally*. I tried to make a great big fortune cookie, but it was so heavy, it collapsed. I even propped up the cookie dough with chopsticks. No luck. Get it? *No luck.*"

"Oh, boy."

"But the good news is—an even BIGGER surprise. You have to see it to believe it. Come out and look in Grandfather Wu's car."

In my wildest dreams, I could never have

imagined good news like this.

A four-foot-long fortune cookie completely filled Grandfather Wu's station wagon. It was golden brown and *absolutely gigantic*.

"Holey moley!" I exclaimed. "How did you make this thing?"

"With stuff I found around the house. When the movers brought Grandfather Wu's china cabinet here from California, they wrapped it in a big sheet of foam. It's been rolled up in the garage. So I cut a big circle out of the foam, used some glue, coat hangers, spray paint and—ta-dah!"

"Our class will love it. It will definitely knock their socks off."

"And guess what? There's even a giant fortune inside."

࿐ ࿐

We could have bought fortune cookies, but we wanted to make our own so we could put our own fortunes inside. We typed the

fortunes on the computer and printed them out. Each fortune was different. Some were funny, some wise, some happy.

By the time we baked the last of the cookies, there was flour in our hair, on our faces and just about everywhere in the kitchen. What a blast.

"We have just enough," I said, "28 cookies total—one for each kid in our class, one for Ms. Mann and one for Grandfather Wu. Perfect."

"The time has come," Ellie said in a serious tone of voice. "We have everything prepared for our speech. Now it's time to practice it."

My knees felt wobbly. But like one of the fortune cookies on our poster board said, "Practice makes perfect."

So we did. Over and over and over again in front of an imaginary audience. Then we filled a plate with chocolate chip cookies to hand out in place of fortune cookies. First we gave our speech to my dog, Benny, who howled at the end for a treat.

Then to my mom and sister, who said we could practice our homework assignments on them any time as long as we brought sweets.

Finally, we did our speech for Grandfather Wu and my dad who were practicing their golf swings in the backyard.

At the end, my dad put his thumb and index finger in his mouth and whistled. Grandfather Wu clapped and said he hoped we got first pick of seats on that luxury bus headed for the Wild and Woolly Mammoth Exhibit.

On Sunday night, my mom tucked me into bed. "You're going to do just fine tomorrow, you know."

"You have to say that. You're my mom."

"No, I'm saying that because it's true. I think you can do anything you put your mind to." She gave me a kiss, turned off the light and whispered "sweet dreams," which is what she says every night of my life.

The moon was so bright that night, it lit up my room. I could see the certificate on my bulletin board from earning last year's Physical Fitness Award. I remembered how the last thing I needed to earn the award was to do the Shuttle Run in just a little over 11 seconds. That seemed *impossible*. But it wasn't. I really, really wanted that award and I put my mind to it.

Next to the award was my summer camp photo. There I was with all the kids in my cabin and my counselors. It was taken on Wacky Wednesday. We were all dressed in kooky outfits and grinning.

You'd never know from that picture that I almost backed out of going to camp. Two weeks seemed too long to be away from my family. But it wasn't. I wanted to sleep in a cabin and make new friends. So I put my mind to it.

Isn't that what Courage really is? Wanting to do something so much that you just put your mind to it and try your very best?

Even if it seems scary or impossible?

If there's one thing I've learned since school started, it's that Things Aren't Always What They Seem. Giving a speech seemed terrifying. But maybe, just maybe, if I put my mind to it, everything would turn out OK.

Looks like I had found my Courage.

Luxury bus here I come.

Chapter Eleven

The highway to happiness is always under construction.

Don't forget that speeches start right after lunch.

Today's Brainteasers:

Think topsy-turvy and fill in the blank:
1. Three peas in a _____
2. She _____ out to the raft.
3. I will _____ the lawn.

Hint, hint: these words are spelled the same way—even if you turn them upside down.

I glanced at the chalkboard. *I think I have all three answers right,* I thought. *Who knows, maybe this will be my lucky day.*

(Maybe it will be yours, too. Go ahead and try the brainteasers on a piece of paper, then check your answers at the end of this book.)

෴ ෴

When I woke up that morning, the first thing I thought of was the speech. I still felt like there was thunder and lightning in my head, but it was a mild storm and passed quickly. And I'll admit that my stomach did feel slightly swirly-whirly. But I was (surprise!) excited.

So was everyone else. In the classroom, there were colorful poster boards filled with pictures, a blue and yellow kite, bags with props* and even a dog bed.

Ellie whispered in my ear, "How's your woofits? Are you aglifft?" (meaning how's your headache...are you scared?)

"I'm OK. Where's the big surprise?"

"Grandfather Wu is bringing it in at one o'clock right before the speeches. He was afraid

87

if he brought it in earlier, someone might eat it for lunch." We giggled.

After lunch, Ms. Mann pulled a piece of paper out of the brain cookie jar. The answer on it was correct (but not mine). Oh well.

She put all the Brainteaser answers in a folder to look through later. Then she dumped little papers with numbers on them into the brain and asked us to take one. "When I call your number, come on up to the front of the room and do your speech."

This is it, I thought, *put your mind to it.*

I had brought the fortune Grandfather Wu had given me. I read it once more, even though I had memorized it. "You're one smart cookie: Face fear, do your best and you'll find success."

Louise's number was called first. She passed around some cute pictures of baby kangaroos peeking out of their mothers' pouches. She ended her speech with my limerick.

Next was Carrie, who answered the

question, "Can you really hear the sound of the ocean in a seashell?" Then Jen gave her speech on "What is a bubble and why is it round?" I had wondered the exact same thing.

Gary's speech was "Why do dogs wag their tails?" He said his dog, Max Junior, is never happier than when he's in his bed. Max Junior made a guest appearance and demonstrated how happiness and tail wagging go together.

Our number was called next. Ellie peeked her head out of the door to tell Grandfather Wu. He had kept the mammoth* fortune cookie in the hallway so it would be a surprise.

I started my part of the speech first. Most of the kids were very surprised to learn that fortune cookies began in America. Then I explained the mystery about who made the first fortune cookie and how the sayings on fortunes were said by different people around the world. I ended by passing out a recipe to everyone.

As I was talking, I could tell kids were really interested—the expressions on their faces said "Really?" and "Wow!" and "Yum!" My three minutes flew by so fast, I didn't even have time to feel swirly-whirly.

Then Ellie spoke about Chinese moon cakes that are part of the Mid-Autumn Festival and how they once held secret messages. She told the class that some people believe when the railroad was first being built, Chinese workers gave each other biscuits with happy sayings inside in place of moon cakes.

I asked if anyone had ever seen a fortune cookie. Of course, everyone's hand went up.

Ellie said, "But have you ever seen one like *this?*" That was Grandfather Wu's signal to bring in the giant cookie and set it on the table in the front of the class. The kids went crazy. I looked at Ms. Mann. She was loving the whole thing.

౨ఆ ఆ౨

They went even crazier when Ellie lifted up the top of the cookie just enough so that

I could reach in and get the tray of fortune cookies we made. Grandfather Wu read a tall tale about fortune cookies while we passed out our homemade treats which, by the way, looked as good as the ones from the Lucky Wow Chow Restaurant.

Then he surprised us all by cracking a few fortune cookie jokes. The kids thought he was hilarious. Grandfather Wu got along with just about anyone.

Ms. Mann must have realized that, too, because after the last speech, she got everyone's attention.

"Class, I'm very proud of the effort each of you made to research, write and give your speech. I'm happy to report that every single person will be going to the Wild and Woolly Mammoth Exhibit on the luxury bus."

Everyone whooped and cheered.

"And one more thing, let's all say thank you to our guest today, Mr. Wu. I wonder if you might consider chaperoning our field trip?"

He nodded his head and smiled.

Now Grandfather Wu wouldn't have just a couple of friends in Pickering Point, he'd have 26, plus the best teacher in the whole school.

Chapter Twelve

Joy is the feeling
of grinning on the inside.

As we were packing up the big cookie to go home, Ellie said, "Hally, I noticed that you didn't get a cookie."

"That's OK, I think Gary took an extra one for Max Junior."

"Well, it just so happens, this cookie was made especially for you." She pointed to the big surprise cookie. "Go ahead. *Get your fortune.*"

I knew she was up to something.

"Barlafumble! Stop!" Grandfather Wu said, just teasing, of course.

"Believe it or not, this is one cookie you *can* open," said Ellie.

I reached my hand into the big, soft, squishy, foam cookie. I pulled out a piece of paper as long as my arm. Leave it to my friend the word lover to make sure there was a message inside.

Eight words were neatly printed in marker:

A very special boonfellow finds a hidden talent.

"I knew you could do it, Hally," said E l l i e . "You were fantabulous."

I guess it was my lucky day after all.

Glossary

*Many words have more than one meaning. Here are the definitions of words marked with this symbol * (an asterisk) as they are used in sentences.*

bigwig: *an important person*
clockwork: *very regularly, predictable*
contagious: *spread from one person to another*
dent: *made smaller or less*
disaster: *an event that causes much damage*
fiasco: *a thing that's a total failure, a big flop*
fiction: *stories or novels about imaginary events and people*
hunky-dory: *going just fine*
inspiration: *something or someone that causes a creative thought or action*
invention: *thinking of or making something that didn't exist before*
lazy Susan: *a tray on a table that spins and holds food*

literally: *understanding words just as they are said, without exaggeration*

mammoth: *a big, hairy elephant that's extinct. It can also mean huge.*

noggin: *head*

noodle: *head*

nutshell: *the least amount of words*

origins: *the place from which something came, the beginning*

philosopher: *an expert in the study of the meaning of life*

progress: *movement forward*

props: *objects used in a performance*

proverb: *an old saying that's true or wise*

rifling: *searching through something in a hurry*

stage fright: *nervous feeling about being in front of a group of people*

stew: *think about troubles, feel anxiety*

superstitions: *beliefs that go against what is generally thought of as true*

tittered: *laughed in a silly way while trying to hold back the sound*

tradition: *an event that has been done for a long time and becomes the usual thing to do*

true-blue: *very loyal*

vile: *disgusting, unpleasant*

visual aids: *objects shown to an audience, used in teaching or speeches*

Yiddish: *a language that developed from an old form of German, spoken by many Jews in Europe, written with the Hebrew alphabet*

Flex Your Mental Muscles

(The answers appear on the next page...no peeking yet!)

Dollars & Sense

1. Imagine that you held up a five-dollar bill and let it fall to the ground five times. How many times would Lincoln's picture face up?

2. How many times does "one" (the word) appear on a one-dollar bill?

Can You Guess?

1. What has teeth but no head?
2. What's never wet, but can be seen in the water?

3. What rock is not a rock?

4. What building has the most stories?

5. Where in the world does Thursday come before Wednesday?

Name That State

You can spell the name of a U.S. state by rearranging the letters of the word "nominates." What state is it?

Riddles & Rhymes

Use these clues and find two words that rhyme. Here's an example:

Color of the sky + narrow boat = blue canoe

1. foolish + nickname for William
2. very large + feline
3. corny + slow
4. circle + dog
5.

Dollars & Sense 1. Five times. Lincoln's picture appears on the front. It's also on the back—he's sitting in front of the Lincoln Memorial in Washington, D.C. 2. Eight times.

Can You Guess? 1. A comb 2. Your reflection 3. A shamrock 4. A library 5. A dictionary

Name That State Minnesota

Rhyming Words 1. Silly Billy 2. Fat Cat 3. Hokey Pokey 4. Round Hound 5. Wild Child

out of control + kid

Answers to Ms. Mann's Brainteasers

Three-Letter Palindromes:
1. The sound of a bursting balloon? POP
2. A joke? GAG
3. What you see with? EYE

Four-, Five- and Seven-Letter Palindromes:
1. A word meaning "look"? PEEP
2. A canoe first made by the Eskimos? KAYAK
3. An auto that goes fast? RACECAR

Homograph Riddle:
1. My doctor was once a PUPIL PUPIL
2. Uncle BILL paid the BILL.
3. All that MINT gum is worth a MINT.

Topsy-Turvy Upside-Down Words:
1. Three peas in a <u>pod</u>
2. She <u>swims</u> out to the raft.
3. I will <u>mow</u> the lawn.

About the Author

Susan Cappadonia Love has written about candy bars, boomerangs, painters and pyramids. She's penned stories about samurai, arithmetic and amazing animal athletes (did you know that a goliath frog can jump nine feet in one leap?). But one of her favorite things having to do with words is reading to her kids at night. Because they can travel around the world, explore real or imaginary places, and get to know people they might not have met. And the best part is—they can do it in their pajamas! The other favorite thing was writing this book (which she also sometimes did in her pajamas, but that's just between us).

She lives in Massachusetts with her husband, Scott, and their two super-duper daughters who go by the names of Sofa Loveseat and Peachie-Pie (but you can call them Sophie and Olivia if you'd prefer).